BEAST QUEST

→ BOOK SEVEN ←

ZEPHA
THE MONSTER SQUID

ADAM BLADE

ILLUSTRATED BY EZRA TUCKER

SCHOLASTIC INC.

New York Toronto London Auckland Sydney
Mexico City New Delhi Hong Kong Buenos Aires

With special thanks to Cherith Baldry

To Rachel Leyshon

ISBN-13: 978-0-545-06863-5
ISBN-10: 0-545-06863-0

Beast Quest series created by Working Partners Ltd., London.
BEAST QUEST is a trademark of Working Partners Ltd.

All rights reserved. Published by Scholastic Inc., 557 Broadway, New York, NY 10012, by arrangement with Working Partners Ltd.

12 11 10 9 8 7 6 5 4   9 10 11 12 13/0

Designed by Tim Hall
Printed in the U.S.A.
First printing, June 2008

KING HUGO'S MASTER OF ARMS PAUSED AT the foot of the stairs. The faint noise of music and laughter could be heard from the Great Hall above. *Thank goodness Avantia is safe again*, he thought, smiling.

The master walked down the stone passage and stopped outside a heavy padded door, studded with brass nails. He pulled a slender golden key from his pocket and held it up. It shone in a ray of light that reached down from an air vent and pierced the gloom of the palace cellars.

The key turned smoothly in the lock. He pushed the door open and stepped into the arms room, closing the door behind him and locking it. As he did so, a ferret poked its head out of his pocket and peered up at him with bright, curious eyes.

"There we are," the master of arms murmured, stroking the ferret's cream-colored fur. "Now no one can get in or out."

The room was so narrow that if the man stretched out his arms, his fingers brushed the walls on either side. Torches blazed in iron holders, casting dancing shadows on the rough stone walls and a few stars shone faintly through the small windows at the top of the back wall.

In the center of the room stood a suit of golden armor. The helmet was dramatically molded into the shape of an eagle's head. The tunic of golden chain mail was covered with a decorated breastplate that shone in the torchlight. Glittering leg armor, gauntlets, and sabatons — armored boots — completed the suit.

The master walked slowly around it, examining each piece with a small grunt of satisfaction. He pulled out a handkerchief to rub a speck of dust from the gleaming breastplate.

"I've looked after this armor for twenty years," he said. "When I first set eyes on it, it took my breath away. And do you know what?" He tickled the ferret's ear. "It still does."

The ferret let out a squeak.

"It's the most precious relic in all of Avantia. We've got to keep every bit of it shining as brightly as the day it was made," he went on. "Its rightful owner could return at any moment." He passed the handkerchief over the smooth curve of the helmet. "We must be ready." He bent down to polish the golden feet of the armor.

Suddenly, the ferret let out a squeal of alarm. Wriggling out of its master's pocket, it dove for a crack in the wall and disappeared.

"Hey!" the man exclaimed. "What's the matter with you?" He straightened up and tried to peer into the crack, but the dancing shadows cast by the torches made it difficult to see. "Come back, you silly creature! There's nothing to be afraid of."

But as he spoke, the shadows began to move, slowly at first, and then with increasing speed. Soon, they were whirling across the walls and floor. He glanced at the torches, but the bright flames burned steadily.

Then something brushed the man's cheek. He spun around at the velvety touch and stared wildly around the room. "These aren't shadows," he said out loud. "They're bats!"

Suddenly, the air was full of black wings. Tiny claws scratched at his face and hands and tangled in his hair.

"No!" He let out a choking cry and beat desperately at the air, trying to drive the creatures back. But the swarming bats still kept coming. He stared in horror at their fierce faces, their eyes glittering with cruel delight.

The master of arms backed toward the door as

more bats squeezed themselves out of cracks in the wall and launched themselves toward him. He felt as if he couldn't breathe.

Soon, the suit of golden armor was covered with bats, hanging from each piece by their hooked claws. With a gasp of horror, the master of arms started forward, but the pain was too much and he collapsed to the floor. Still he kept on struggling, trying with all his might to drag himself toward the precious armor.

"Stop!" he gasped. "Help! Somebody, help!"

But it was too late. Bats covered the man's head and back, clinging to his hair and suffocating him with their wings. He felt as if every last scrap of air was being pressed out of his lungs, and stared in disbelief as the golden armor rose slowly into the air, lifted by the evil swarm of bats. Only the wooden stand was left.

Then darkness flooded over him.

⊷ Chapter One ⊶

Gone!

T OM STOOD NEXT TO A PILLAR IN THE GREAT
Hall of King Hugo's palace and watched the
dancing. He was elated to see all the king's subjects
celebrating the end of his Quest. Their silk
and satin robes shone as they whirled in the
afternoon sun.

King Hugo watched from the High Table
with a contented smile. Tom knew he was happy
that the six Beasts of Avantia had been released
from the evil spell of the Dark Wizard, Malvel.
Ferno the Fire Dragon, Sepron the Sea Serpent,
Cypher the Mountain Giant, Tagus the Night
Horse, Tartok the Ice Beast, and Epos the Winged

Flame were now protecting the kingdom instead of destroying it. Avantia could begin to recover.

But Tom couldn't join in the celebration. Something had been nagging at him ever since that final meeting with Malvel on the mountainside in the far east of the kingdom. He told himself over and over again that Malvel had fallen into the volcano and perished in its raging fires.

But he couldn't forget what Malvel had screamed at him as he fell: *"This is not the end, Tom! We shall meet again!"*

Tom had a horrible feeling that he had not seen the last of his enemy. Then he remembered the hooded figure he had spotted in the cheering crowd when he returned from freeing Epos, the last of the cursed Beasts. If the Dark Wizard had indeed survived, how would he take revenge for his defeat?

Tom shuddered. He wished his father, Taladon the Swift, were here. He had been a knight and had undertaken a Beast Quest of his own. Only he could know how Tom felt. But no one had seen him for many years. It was as if he had disappeared into thin air, although Tom felt certain that they would meet again one day.

Tom felt a hand on his shoulder. He turned to see Elenna, the friend who had shared every step of the Quest with him. She was wearing a dress of blue silk, but her untidy, short dark hair stuck out, just as when they'd first met.

"What's the matter, Tom?" she asked. "Why are you looking so worried?"

Tom shook his head uneasily. "I'm not sure . . . I just keep remembering the last thing that Malvel said on the mountain."

"Malvel is finished," Elenna declared. "There's nothing to worry about." Taking Tom's hand, she dragged him toward the dance floor. "I've just been to the stables. Storm is stuffing himself with the best apples, and look — Silver's enjoying himself under the table there."

Tom smiled as he saw the wolf contentedly gnawing on a bone, and was glad to think of his black stallion enjoying a well-deserved rest in the comfortable palace stables.

"Everyone's happy," Elenna went on. "Can't you be happy, too? Let's dance."

"I don't know how to dance," Tom said, laughing.

To Tom's relief, the music stopped before Elenna had the chance to persuade him.

Then he spotted King Hugo's wizard and adviser, Aduro, making his way toward them. They would never have completed the Quest if it hadn't been for the good wizard, who had helped and encouraged them in their most difficult moments. Now he wore a magnificent embroidered robe and carried a polished wooden staff in one hand. Tom bowed, and Elenna dropped into a deep curtsy.

"Are you enjoying yourselves?" Aduro asked.

"Yes, it's wonderful!" Elenna's eyes sparkled.

The wizard smiled. "If you don't mind missing some of the dancing, I've got something to show you. Something in the palace cellars."

"Not more danger?" Tom was instantly alert.

Aduro shook his head, smiling, and Tom realized that even the king's adviser thought Malvel had been defeated for good. "No," the wizard replied. "It's a reward for a successful Quest. Avantia owes you a great deal."

Tom and Elenna followed him to a small door at the far end of the hall and down a long flight of stairs. Elenna was bouncing with excitement.

At the foot of the steps was a narrow passage. Aduro led them on, then stopped outside a padded door. A single shaft of light shone down from a high air vent and gleamed on the door's brass nails and lock.

"This is strange," the wizard said. "I was expecting to meet the king's master of arms here. He's not the sort of man to be late. I wonder what has happened to him?"

"Maybe he's inside," Elenna suggested.

Aduro turned the door handle, but the door remained shut. "Locked," he muttered. "Maybe —"

He broke off at the sound of a loud groan coming from inside the room. Tom and Elenna exchanged a glance.

"It sounds as if someone's hurt," said Tom.

Wizard Aduro laid the end of his staff against the lock and commanded, "Open!"

The lock clicked and the door swung open. Inside the room, an elderly man lay sprawled on the floor. A ferret was nosing at him anxiously. The old man tried to get up, but his strength gave way and he slumped down again.

Tom and Elenna ran to his side. He was barely conscious. His face was pale, his black tunic was

torn, and his face and hands were covered with tiny bites and scratches.

Tom helped the old man to sit up.

"Aduro, can you magic a jug of water for him?" Elenna asked. "Quickly!"

But the wizard simply stared at the space in the middle of the room, empty except for a wooden armor stand. He didn't seem to have heard Elenna's anxious plea. He looked stunned.

Tom jumped to his feet. "What's the matter?" he asked.

Aduro turned to him, blinking as if he were just waking up. "Something terrible has happened." His voice was hoarse. "The golden armor. It's gone!"

CHAPTER TWO

A NEW QUEST

"CAN YOU TELL US WHAT HAPPENED?" ADURO asked, kneeling beside the injured man.

The master of arms drew in a shaky breath. "Bats!" he whispered. "The whole room was full of bats. They took the armor." He covered his face with his hands. "I have failed the king."

Aduro touched the old man's shoulder. "No, my friend. Evil has been at work here." Standing up again, he thumped on the floor three times with his staff.

A moment later, Tom heard running footsteps in the passage, and two servants appeared in the doorway. Their eyes grew wide with shock as they looked inside.

"Carry the master to his room," Wizard Aduro ordered. "Send for King Hugo's healer. And say nothing of what you've seen to anyone."

The two servants lifted the elderly man carefully. Elenna scooped up the ferret and gave it to him as he was carried out into the passage.

As soon as the master of arms and the servants were gone, Tom turned to the wizard. "This was Malvel's work! It must have been. He is still alive after all."

Aduro nodded gravely. "I fear that you are right."

"What armor was he talking about?" Elenna asked. "Why is it so important?"

"Tom, the armor was to have been your reward for completing the Quest," Aduro explained. "Once it belonged to the Master of the Beasts. It brings magical strengths to its rightful owner."

"But . . ." Tom was puzzled. "You couldn't give me the armor if it belongs to the Master of the Beasts. I remember you told me that Malvel had imprisoned him long before my Quest began, but why isn't he still wearing it?"

Aduro let out a long sigh. "Many years ago, the Master of the Beasts should have returned to the palace for the New Year feast. Instead, the empty suit of armor appeared in the Great Hall as the nobles were taking their places." The wizard paused, then went on. "Malvel had captured him, then sent the armor to mock King Hugo — and me."

Tom felt as if an icy hand had clutched his heart. He hoped the Master of the Beasts had not suffered too greatly in the hands of the Dark Wizard.

"However, I felt that all was not lost," Aduro said. "The powers of the armor would still work if the suit was worn by the right person — a true Quester with brave blood running through his veins. I think you are that person, Tom."

For a moment Tom could not speak. He wasn't sure he was worthy to wear the golden armor. But he would give everything to protect Avantia.

The wizard began to pace impatiently back and forth in the small room, his staff clicking on the stone floor. "Malvel must have realized that your successful Quest has made you a danger to him. He would never have imagined that anyone — much less a boy — could lift the spells on all six Beasts. He has stolen the armor to stop *you* from wearing it and gaining its magical powers."

"But it would never fit me." Tom measured himself against the wooden stand that had held the armor. "It must have been made for a tall man."

"This armor will always fit he who serves the Beasts," Aduro explained. "Its magic can sense it."

"Then we have to do something!" Elenna's eyes sparkled with indignation. "We can't let Malvel get away with this."

More cautiously, Tom added, "But what has Malvel done with it? Can he use it for himself?"

Aduro halted in his pacing. "No, he cannot. But perhaps we can see something of where it has gone." He raised his staff and swept it in a wide arc. The air glittered in its wake and a picture gradually formed, hovering in the air.

Tom and Elenna let out gasps of wonder and fear.

They could see a multitude of flying bats, carrying pieces of the golden armor hooked in their claws. Then the swarm split up. Groups of bats flew off in six different directions, each carrying a piece of the armor. The sound of Malvel's mocking laughter grew until it filled the room.

Then the vision faded. When it had gone, Aduro let out a weary sigh. "This is worse than I feared.

Malvel's bats have scattered the armor around the kingdom." He looked gravely at Tom. "Are you ready for another Quest, so soon after your first? Will you seek out the pieces of armor and bring them back together?"

Tom drew himself up. "Of course I will."

"And what about me?" Elenna asked with a fierce look. "Where Tom goes, I go!"

A relieved smile spread over Aduro's face. "Thank you, Elenna. I know that you, too, have the courage to succeed. The magic map will once again show you where to go. Fetch it and change into your traveling clothes. Meet me in the stables as soon as you can."

Tom hurried back to his room and changed into a woolen tunic and thick cloak. He fastened on his scabbard, sheathed his sword, and picked up his shield. It bore the six magical tokens from the Beasts he had already freed: Ferno's dragon scale protected him from heat, Sepron's tooth from rushing water, Cypher's eagle feather from great heights, and Tartok's claw from extreme cold. Tagus's horseshoe fragment gave him extra speed and Epos's golden feather healed wounds.

Surely their combined power would strengthen him now?

Then Tom went down to the stables. As he crossed the courtyard Elenna caught up with him, Silver at her heels.

"I took some leftover food from the feast," she said, showing Tom a large bundle wrapped in a white cloth.

"Good thinking," Tom said, smiling. It wouldn't hurt to have a few days' supplies on-hand.

Aduro was waiting in the stables. A groom had already saddled Storm. Elenna stroked the stallion's nose and fed him one last apple.

Tom carefully placed the map in one of Storm's saddlebags. The wizard glanced at the familiar parchment scroll. "Guard the map well. And take care. This time, Malvel knows you are a threat to him. His magic is clearly as strong as ever, and now he is angry."

"I'm not afraid of Malvel," Tom said bravely, resting his hand on the hilt of his sword.

Storm snorted, rapping one hoof against the stable floor, and Silver let out a howl of agreement, but Aduro's face was creased with concern.

Tom climbed into Storm's saddle and Elenna scrambled up behind him.

"Farewell," said Aduro. "And may good luck go with you."

He ordered the guards to open the gates of the palace.

Tom urged Storm into a trot. As they passed through the gates, with Silver bounding alongside, Tom could still hear music and sounds of celebration ringing out from the palace walls. The rest of Avantia had no idea that Malvel was alive and plotting once more.

Tom was determined that the Dark Wizard would not succeed. He and Elenna would follow this new Quest to the end.

CHAPTER THREE

MALVEL'S WARNING

"I'M GLAD I'M NOT ALONE ON THIS QUEST," Tom told Elenna as they rode away from the palace. "I know we can do this together."

"Silver and Storm will help us, too," Elenna said. "And don't forget the Beasts. They're friendly now, and it's their job to protect Avantia. Maybe we can call on them to help us fight Malvel."

"That's true," said Tom, feeling a swell of determination. With Elenna, their animal friends, and the Beasts of Avantia on his side, he knew that it was his destiny to defeat Malvel.

The road they were following led through fields where cattle grazed peacefully. A few trees grew here and there in the lush grass; the afternoon sun cast long shadows.

Soon they came to a crossroads. Tom brought Storm to a halt and pulled out Wizard Aduro's enchanted map. As he unrolled it a red path began to glow, leading to the coast.

"That's the road we took when we met Sepron the Sea Serpent." Elenna pointed out, peering over Tom's shoulder.

"Then at least we know the way." Tom rolled up the map, put it back in the saddlebag, and urged Storm on.

They passed through a narrow belt of trees and began to climb a hill. Tom noticed that the sunlight was growing hazy, as though night was falling. A chill wind whispered over him. But the sun still stood well above the horizon, and the sky was blue except for a few puffs of white clouds. Tom glanced around, uneasy. He couldn't see anything except trees and fields.

Then he looked up. High above in the blue sky, black dots were flitting back and forth. Tom remembered the vision Aduro had shown them. "Bats!" he exclaimed.

He felt Elenna lock her arms tightly around his waist. "I thought bats only flew at night," she said.

"Malvel bent the great Beasts to his will. It must be easy to get bats to do his bidding," Tom replied grimly.

He reined Storm in and gripped the hilt of his sword, ready to draw it. The black stallion threw his head up and his harness jingled. Beside the horse, Silver stood stiff-legged, barking angrily at the sky.

The bats flew lower and lower, until they were swooping around Tom and Elenna. Storm snorted nervously; Tom patted his neck to reassure him. Silver leaped into the air, his jaws snapping vainly at the leathery wings.

Tom and Elenna had to duck to avoid the

creatures' talons. Tom didn't dare try to outrun them on Storm; the path was steep and rough, and the stallion could easily be injured. In a desperate move, he drew his sword and slashed at the whirling pack of bats. They fluttered upward out of range and then clustered together in a rolling ball.

Elenna gasped in astonishment. "What are they doing?"

Slowly, the ball took on a different shape. Icy fear rushed through Tom as he recognized the hooded being that had laughed at him so cruelly on that mountainside. It stretched across half the sky, from above Tom's head to the distant horizon.

"Malvel!" he exclaimed.

The Dark Wizard was using the bats to give form to his evil face. Tom could see the gleam of his sunken eyes and the twisted line of his cruel mouth. Mocking laughter poured out and Malvel's voice boomed around them.

"I hope you enjoyed my surprise. You are fools if you think you can defeat me!"

Tom raised his sword. "I *know* we can defeat you. We'll track down every piece of the armor that you have stolen. Nothing is going to stop us!"

Malvel's laughter echoed again. "Nothing? Not even *new* Beasts with evil hearts? Beasts that I have created?"

For a moment Tom was shocked into silence.

Silver let out a miserable whine, and hurled himself into the air again, snapping at Malvel's shape.

"New Beasts!" Elenna exclaimed. "What do you mean?"

Malvel replied. "You'll find out soon enough, when you meet Zepha. Maybe then you'll change your minds."

"Never!" Tom cried defiantly. "You can conjure up whatever Beasts you like, but they won't stop me. I'll never fail Avantia!"

But who — or what — was Zepha? Tom felt a lurch of fear in the pit of his stomach as he thought of the six new Beasts he would have to face.

Then the bats began to scatter. Malvel's face broke up and disappeared, but his jeering laughter echoed around the hills until every last bat had vanished.

Tom sheathed his sword. His stomach was still churning. Elenna looked white and shaken, Storm was sweating and trembling, and Silver's tail was dragging in the dust of the road.

"I think we should make camp," Tom said, trying to keep his voice firm. "The sun's going down and it'll be dark soon."

Elenna nodded in agreement. They dismounted, and Tom led the way to a small clump of trees not far from the road. There was a pool in the middle of the trees, at the bottom of a rocky hollow. Tom unsaddled Storm while Elenna collected wood and made a fire. They were both glad of the bright flames as the sun sank lower and darkness began to creep around them.

Elenna unpacked the food she had saved from the feast and handed Tom some bread and cold chicken. "I wonder why Aduro didn't warn us about the new Beasts," she said.

"Perhaps he didn't know," Tom replied. "This is a different Quest. This time we're on our own."

Elenna's eyes shone with steely resolve. "We'll manage," she said. "We've got to."

When they had finished eating, Tom wrapped himself in his cloak and lay down beside the remains of the fire. He gazed up, searching. The moon shone brightly behind wisps of cloud; no black specks dotted the sky and the wind carried no sound of leathery wings.

But now Tom knew that something else was out there. Something even more dangerous than Malvel's vicious bats.

A new set of evil Beasts.

Maybe they were already circling around him, hidden by the night. Tom peered into the shadows, but he couldn't see anything.

It took a long time for sleep to come.

CHAPTER FOUR

DANGER AT SEA

BY NOON THE NEXT DAY, THEY WERE DRAWING near the coast. Tom remembered how they had struggled through the floodwaters that Sepron the Sea Serpent had caused. Now the land was clear again: Gardens were growing and houses had been repaired with new wood and thatch. Tom felt proud that Avantia was safe again, but couldn't help but worry what could lay in store if Malvel carried out his evil plans.

At last the road led Tom and his friends through a patch of thin woodland and out onto the shore.

"Look!" exclaimed Elenna, pointing. "All the

fishermen's huts have been rebuilt. And there are lots of new boats."

At first Tom was pleased to see the snug new huts and the brightly painted fishing boats pulled up on the beach, with fishing nets piled up beside them. Then he frowned.

"Shouldn't all those boats be out at sea?" he asked. He exchanged an uncertain glance with Elenna. "What's going on here?"

"There's a smell of dead fish, too," said Elenna, wrinkling her nose.

Tom spotted a wisp of smoke rising from behind some boulders farther along the beach. He and Elenna dismounted. Leaving Storm to crop the grass under the trees, they headed for the rocks. As they drew closer they saw a group of people crouched around a driftwood fire. One woman was ladling stew from an iron pot into wooden bowls. All the people looked worried and miserable.

Then Tom recognized a tall boy with red hair and a freckled face. "Calum!" he exclaimed.

The boy looked up and sprang to his feet. "Tom!" He hugged Tom and then Elenna, before bending down to plunge his hands into the thick fur around Silver's neck. "It's good to see you again."

"It's good to see you, too," Tom said. He would never forget how Calum had helped him when he came to free Sepron the Sea Serpent from Malvel's evil spell.

"What's going on here?" Elenna asked.

"Yes, why is no one out in the boats?" Tom added.

The men and women around the fire exchanged nervous glances.

"It's too dangerous to go out to sea," Calum explained after a moment's hesitation. "A couple of our people didn't come back yesterday. We found wreckage washed up onshore, but no one knows what happened to the boatmen."

Tom glanced swiftly at Elenna. She was looking as confused as he felt. Sepron was free now, and should have been protecting this part of the kingdom. What had gone wrong?

"Do you know why they disappeared?" he asked Calum.

A man Tom recognized as Calum's father, Matt, pointed out to sea. "Whirlpools," he said. "They appeared a few days ago near those rocks. No one knows why. Only a fool would go out there now."

"Or Lindon," another man said with a bitter laugh.

"Who's Lindon?" Tom asked.

"A stubborn fool," the man replied.

"He doesn't know what's good for him," a woman chimed in. "He insisted on going out this morning, trawling for fish, just as he always does. He hasn't returned yet."

"And goodness knows why he went," Calum's father added grumpily. "The pickings are thin enough. Since the whirlpools appeared, all the fish have gone."

"Some of them have washed up dead," Calum said, pointing to the edge of the water.

Tom could see the gleam of silver fish lying amongst the other debris. Silver trotted down to the water's edge and snuffled at one of them. Then he drew back with a disgusted snort.

"Silver! Here, boy." Elenna tickled the wolf's ears as he returned to her. "Be careful where you put your nose."

"These were good fishing waters," the woman went on. "But if the whirlpools stay, we'll have nothing but a few vegetables to live on."

Tom gazed at Calum. The boy's eyes were filled with hope. He was the only one from this village who knew that Tom had freed Sepron from Malvel's curse.

"I think I might know something about this,"

Tom said softly, so that only Calum could hear. "Wait here."

Beckoning to Elenna, he hurried back to where they had left Storm. He pulled the magic map out of the saddlebag. When he unrolled it, he could see a picture of a golden helmet resting in the sea beside a rocky islet.

"That's exactly where the whirlpools are," said Elenna.

Tom met her anxious gaze. His pulse began to race with a mixture of fear and excitement.

"You heard what Calum said," Elenna went on. "Boats that go out there don't come back."

Tom gazed out across the waves. "I don't have a choice," he said. "This is my Quest. I have to go."

CHAPTER FIVE

LINDON

Tom put the map back into one of Storm's saddlebags. As he turned to the shore once again, he spotted a fishing boat sailing around a headland toward the beach, its white sail billowing.

"That must be Lindon," he said. "Maybe he'll take us out to the whirlpools in his boat. Come on!"

Tom and Elenna hurried down to the water's edge, Silver and Storm trotting behind.

The boat soon reached the beach, and the fisherman leaped out and pulled it up beside the other vessels. He lifted a reed basket out of the boat, but Tom could see there were only a few fish in the bottom.

"Are you Lindon?" Tom asked.

"That's me." The fisherman dumped his basket on the beach and straightened up. He was a tall young man with shaggy dark hair. His face was harsh and unfriendly. "Who wants to know?"

"I do. I need to go out to sea. Will you take me?"

"I might, if the price is right," Lindon replied. "Where do you want to go?"

"Over there." Tom pointed out toward the rocky islet.

Lindon raised his eyebrows. "There are whirlpools out there. That will cost extra."

Tom exchanged a glance with Elenna. "I can't afford to pay you," he began, "but —"

"That's all right." Tom realized that Lindon was staring past him at Silver. "I'd accept a trade. I'll take that mutt off your hands."

Elenna stepped in front of the wolf. She looked furious at the suggestion that she would hand over her faithful friend. The hair on Silver's spine rose up and he let out a soft growl.

"We can't do that," Tom said firmly. "Isn't there something else you want? Or anything we could do for you?"

Lindon narrowed his eyes. "Why do you want to go out there, anyway?" he asked.

Tom knew he couldn't tell anyone about his Quest. The first time had been bad enough, with the good Beasts of Avantia under terrible curses. But now that Malvel had unleashed his own evil Beasts on the kingdom, it was even more urgent to keep the Quest a secret. The people of Avantia would panic if they knew what the Dark Wizard was up to. "I have something important to do," he said.

Lindon let out a bark of rough laughter.

"'Something important?' You'll have to let on more than that if you want my help."

Tom saw that Elenna was red with anger on his behalf. He had to act quickly before she said something they would both regret.

The people of the village did say that Lindon liked to take risks. Maybe he would help if he thought that Tom was equally reckless.

"I want to see if I can survive diving into a whirlpool," Tom said, thinking quickly. "And I've also heard the fish are dying. Maybe I can discover what's causing it."

Lindon looked at him with astonishment for a moment. Then he shook his head and laughed. "Well, you're a mad one, make no mistake," he said, then paused, a sly look passing over his face. "If you don't come back, I'll have your fine-looking horse." He nodded to Storm, who pawed the ground anxiously. "If you do make it, I'll just shake you by the hand and wish you well." He sighed. "Who knows? Maybe you can find out what is killing the fish. We'll all starve if it continues."

Tom stroked Storm's neck. "Don't worry, boy, I'll be back," he said reassuringly, but he couldn't ignore the swelling fear in his stomach.

Tom had faced danger in this ocean before. But now he *had* to defeat Zepha and find the golden helmet. If he didn't, he would lose his horse as well as his life. Not to mention leaving the golden armor in Malvel's evil grasp.

→ CHAPTER SIX ←

OUT TO SEA

"I'M COMING WITH YOU," ELENNA SAID, AS Lindon got the boat ready.

"No," Tom told her. "Not this time. I couldn't have freed Sepron without you. But defeating Zepha and finding the helmet is something I have to do on my own."

Elenna bit her lip, then nodded, understanding. Tom unfastened his scabbard and handed it to her.

"You might need this," he said. "And my shield is tied to Storm's saddle. The people here are desperate; they might be dangerous. And you never know what Malvel might do."

Elenna hesitated. "But won't you need your sword and shield?" she asked.

Tom knew he would be vulnerable without them — but there was no way he was leaving Elenna with just her bow and quiver of arrows. He'd have to rely on his wits. He took Elenna's hand and wrapped her fingers around the hilt of his sword. "I'll be fine," he told her.

"I'll stay with Calum and his father," she said. "I've nothing to fear from them. But, Tom, be careful. Remember what Malvel said about Zepha."

Cold fear gripped Tom again. He didn't even know what Zepha *was*. How could he prepare to fight an evil Beast when he had no idea what it looked like?

"Are you coming or not?" Lindon's harsh voice interrupted his thoughts.

"I'm coming," said Tom, pushing down his apprehension.

Elenna grasped his hand. "Good luck," she said.

Silver added an encouraging bark and Storm whinnied.

"Don't worry. I'll be back soon," Tom promised.

He helped Lindon push the boat back into the water and scrambled over the side. The sky was covered with thick, gray clouds. Lindon raised the sail, and soon the boat was scudding over the waves again. Tom looked back at the shore where Elenna, Silver, and Storm stood. Already they seemed very small and distant.

As Lindon steered the boat out to sea, the wind grew even stronger. The water became choppy and the boat pitched up and down on the waves.

Tom gripped the side and stared down into the sea. He thought he could make out the movement of some dark shape far beneath the surface. Suddenly, the water began to churn angrily and Tom gasped as he realized that the boat was

swirling around in a huge circle. A whirlpool was starting up — and he and Lindon were at the center of it!

Memories of the deep, green water and the feeling of his chest straining for air bubbled up from Tom's mind. He had faced Sepron in these very waters — and nearly drowned in the process.

Lindon laughed. "Getting scared?" he taunted. "Do you want to change your mind?"

"No!" Tom was determined not to let Lindon see he was afraid. "This is what I've come for."

Lindon grunted and deftly steered the boat out of the whirlpool. Tom could tell he was a skillful sailor. Even so, the boat rocked dangerously and water slopped over the side, soaking Tom. Lindon guided the boat to the edge of the churning water. "I'll wait for you here," he said. "But don't take too long! Otherwise I'll be heading back to collect your horse."

Tom climbed onto the side of the boat. The water was circling faster than ever, opening a cone-shaped passage into the depths of the sea. Tom's heart thumped in terror, but he knew he couldn't turn back. Another memory struggled to the surface now, stronger than the others: sunlight on the sea, air rushing into his lungs, and the tooth of a sea serpent in his hand. When Tom had dove into the sea to meet Sepron, he had emerged victorious.

"I have to do this," Tom muttered. "For the golden armor. And to defeat Malvel."

Tom took in a lungful of air and closed his mouth tightly. Then he dove off the boat's edge.

⇥ CHAPTER SEVEN ⇤

INTO THE WHIRLPOOL

THE WHIRLPOOL SUCKED TOM DOWN INTO THE depths of the ocean at once. The force of the water dragged at his clothes and wrenched his arms and legs. Tom felt as if he were being torn apart.

Swirling water was all around him. Caught up in the powerful current, Tom spun around and around. He fought not to lose his bearings, but soon he couldn't tell whether he was facing up toward the surface of the sea or down to the ocean bed.

I'm going to drown! he thought frantically. Was this the end of his new Quest already?

Then pain stabbed through him as his flailing

arm struck something hard. Instinctively, he grabbed at it and found he was clinging to a spur of rock that thrust upward from the ocean bed. Working his way along it, he managed to drag himself out from the force of the whirlpool and up to the surface. He took a few deep breaths to calm his panic, and dove back down once more.

Looking around, Tom saw the spires and hollows of a coral bed stretching into the distance. Then a dull gleam of gold caught his eye. On one spike of coral rested the golden helmet.

He had never seen a helmet like it before. It was shaped like an eagle's head: The visor was molded in the shape of a hooked beak, and the golden surface was patterned to look like feathers.

Tom was amazed. He couldn't believe how easy this was! He would just collect the helmet, then swim back up to the boat.

Kicking away from the rock, Tom swam toward the golden gleam. But as he reached for the helmet, he spotted movement just beyond it. A dark shadow was rising up from behind the coral. It was so huge that it took Tom a moment to realize it was a head, with staring, bulging eyes and a mouth like a gaping beak. Seconds later, a body followed, a mass of giant tentacles. Tom could see through the creature's skin, to where three red hearts were pumping.

Zepha was a giant squid! More than that, a *monster* squid!

This was the Beast who was threatening the villagers with starvation by driving all the fish away. Panic froze him. How could he battle such a vast creature? His eyes alone were as tall as Tom was and his beak could swallow him up in one bite.

Before Tom could make a dive for the helmet, the squid hurtled out of its shelter in the coral, its snaking tentacles lashing out for Tom.

Tom felt his lungs start to hurt with the effort of

holding his breath. As he pushed himself through the water, away from the grasping tentacles, he let the last few precious bubbles of air escape from his mouth.

Now he was deep below the surface with no air, and the monster squid was between him and the helmet.

What could he do now? He'd never get out alive!

CHAPTER EIGHT

UNEXPECTED HELP

KICKING OUT STRONGLY, TOM SWAM FOR THE surface — fast. At any moment, he expected one of Zepha's tentacles to fasten around his ankle, dragging him back into the depths.

Tom's head burst through the surface of the sea; he coughed up water and took in great gulps of air. Blinking to clear his eyes, he spotted Lindon's boat rocking on the waves a few yards away, and swam carefully around the whirlpool toward it. When he reached the boat, Lindon leaned over the side to help him on board.

"I thought I'd seen the last of you," said Lindon.

There was a grudging respect in his tone of voice. He grasped Tom's hand and shook it firmly. "I reckon you can keep your horse after that." He looked at Tom curiously. "What did you see down there?"

"You have to take me back!" Tom gasped. "I need to pick up Elenna."

Lindon saw the determination in his face and nodded. Quickly he hauled on the ropes and soon the boat was plunging back toward the beach.

Elenna was waiting for Tom at the water's edge, holding his sword and shield. She flung them down and hugged Tom as he leaped ashore. Silver bounded around him excitedly, letting out a howl of welcome.

"You're safe!" Elenna exclaimed. "But where's the helmet?"

"At the bottom of the sea," Tom replied. "Guarded by a giant squid."

"Zepha is a squid?"

"Yes. He's huge. A monster." Hesitating, he added, "I'm not sure I can defeat him."

"Then we can do it together," Elenna said.

Tom was warmed by his friend's courage and loyalty. "I was hoping you'd say that," he said.

He turned back to Lindon, only to see the fisherman already heading away, toward the people still huddled around the fire. He was carrying the basket of fish he had caught earlier.

"Hey!" Tom called out. "I need you to take me out there again."

"I've had more than my share of risk for today," Lindon said. He shook his head regretfully. "I'm not going back out again. Sorry." He strode off toward the fire.

Elenna and Tom looked at each other. They both knew that Elenna was skillful at handling a boat.

"Do you think we should take it?" Elenna whispered.

"We had to do that last time, when we freed Sepron," Tom replied. "It's for the good of the people here. We have no choice."

When they were sure that no one was looking, Tom fastened on his scabbard and put his shield into the boat. Then he and Elenna climbed in. Silver watched them, letting out a mournful whine.

"All right, you can come, too," said Elenna.

The wolf's ears went up and he took a flying leap into the boat, which rocked from side to side.

"Storm will be fine," Elenna added. "Calum is looking after him."

Tom's fear returned as Elenna guided the boat out to sea. He imagined one of Zepha's giant tentacles lashing out of the water, dragging the boat down into the depths. All three of them would drown.

"Are you ready for this? It's very dangerous. . . ." he began.

"We wanted to come, didn't we, Silver?" Elenna said calmly.

Silver gave a yelp of agreement.

"But you haven't *seen* Zepha." Had he made a mistake coming back for his friend?

"I've seen Sepron, though," Elenna said. "If we could defeat him, we can defeat Zepha."

"Sepron!" Tom shouted. "Of course!"

Tom grabbed his shield and polished Sepron's tooth hard with the sleeve of his tunic. At first nothing happened. Then, Tom heard the sound of rushing water.

Elenna leaned over the side. "I can see something moving!" she cried.

Tom's stomach lurched. "Sepron?" he asked himself. "Or Zepha?"

Joy flooded through him as a huge head and arching neck burst out of the water, glittering

seawater pouring off it. Tom gazed up at Sepron's shining eyes and rainbow-colored scales.

"It worked!" Elenna laughed.

The great sea serpent arched his neck protectively over the boat. Then he dove beneath the waves again. Even though Tom could no longer see him, he knew that the Beast was there, ready to help and protect them. Would it be enough? Or was Malvel's evil Beast too strong, even for Sepron?

As if in answer to Tom's question, a blue glow formed in the air just ahead of the boat. Inside it, Aduro appeared. Tom could still see the tossing waves through his robes. The wizard had sent an illusion of himself, just as he had many times before.

"Don't give up hope, Tom," he said.

Tom smiled, happy to see such a familiar face. "Aduro!"

"I don't have much time, so I'll speak quickly. It was good thinking to summon Sepron," Aduro went on. "But remember: As a good Beast of Avantia, he can only attack Zepha in order to protect you."

Tom nodded in understanding. He had so many questions, but the wizard's form was already beginning to fade.

"Good luck!" Aduro called out before he disappeared altogether. Then the blue mist evaporated, and Tom could see the turbulent water at the edge of the whirlpool.

Silver began to whine and pace back and forth along the boards of the boat.

"He knows something's wrong," Elenna said grimly.

Gripping his shield, Tom climbed onto the side of the boat, Elenna scrambling up beside him.

"I'll distract Zepha," Tom said. "When he comes

after me, you grab the helmet and swim back to the boat as fast as you can."

Elenna nodded.

Tom gazed down into the whirlpool. Just below the surface Sepron was circling, waiting.

"Stay, Silver," Elenna told the wolf. He whimpered a little, but settled down obediently in the bottom of the boat with his nose on his paws.

"This is it," Tom said.

Together, he and Elenna dove into the whirlpool.

CHAPTER NINE

THE ANGER OF ZEPHA

THIS TIME THE WEIGHT OF TOM'S SWORD AND shield took him down faster. He managed to keep his sense of direction, swimming in a spiral down to the seabed. He looked up. Above him, Elenna swam with Sepron.

Soon Tom spotted the coral reef and the golden glint of the helmet. He pointed Elenna toward it. Elenna saw his signal and began to head in that direction.

Then the huge form of Zepha came into view behind the spires of coral. Tom saw Elenna's mouth open in a cry of horror. Valuable air bubbled away toward the surface. Tom had to help! He swam close to her and gripped her shoulder encouragingly.

Then they swam on together toward the menacing shape of the monster squid.

As they drew closer, Tom could see the giant tentacles waving gently in the underwater tide. Zepha was curled up as if he was sleeping. But Tom wasn't fooled.

In a sudden movement, Elenna darted toward the helmet. Tom swam nearer, despite the danger, hoping to distract the evil Beast. But he got too close.

As Tom turned to swim away, hoping Zepha would be lured to follow, a tentacle lashed out and wrapped itself around his ankle.

Tom tugged furiously, trying to free himself. He spotted Elenna swimming in his direction, but waved her back, toward the helmet.

He could feel the tentacle tightening. It was cutting off his blood supply; his foot was growing numb. He kicked out, trying to swim for the surface, but the tentacle held him back. Starting to panic, Tom swallowed a mouthful of seawater and began to choke. Then he caught another glimpse of Elenna. Her knife in her hand, she was swimming down toward the giant squid. She pulled her arm back, and the knife flashed in a shaft of sunlight that pierced the sea-green gloom. Then she thrust the blade deep into the tough muscle of Zepha's tentacle.

The Beast's pale eyes opened wide in a spasm of pain and fury. Tom felt the grip on his ankle loosen. Drawing his sword, he slashed angrily at the tentacle. Red blood billowed out into the water. The tip of the tentacle fell away as the Beast thrashed wildly in agony. Tom was free — for the moment.

He swam away from Zepha, but the squid heaved himself up from the coral bed and gave chase, closing the gap between himself and Tom with frightening speed.

Then Tom saw Sepron swimming toward them. His scales glittered and his eyes flashed with fury. The sea serpent's jaws gaped as he snapped angrily at Zepha. His teeth punctured the squid's leathery skin and gripped tightly.

Zepha twisted with rage and pain, and squirted a huge cloud of black ink from the underside of his body into the sea serpent's face. Sepron reared back, blinded by the ink and lashing his head from side to side as the black cloud spread. His grip on Zepha loosened as he rolled over and over in the water, trying to clear his sight.

Free again, the monster squid shot after Tom. His tentacles thrashed through the sea, churning up underwater currents. Tom was battered around by the angry water. Where was Elenna? He couldn't see her! He swiped at Zepha with his sword, aiming at the three hearts that pulsed beneath the squid's skin.

But one flailing tentacle knocked the sword

out of his hand. Tom stared in horror as it sank and was lost in the darkness of the green, watery depths.

Tom had never felt so alone. Sepron couldn't help him, and Elenna had vanished. His arms and legs ached with exhaustion, and the air in his lungs was running out again. He struck out for the surface, but he knew he would never swim fast enough to escape, and he had no weapon left to fight the monster.

Zepha sensed Tom's weakness and swam right for him, his beak open wide. The beast's pale eyes gleamed. One of his tentacles coiled around Tom's waist. Terrified, Tom felt himself dragged closer to the gaping hole of the squid's mouth. He held up his shield as a last attempt to defend himself. But Zepha's mouth was big enough to engulf the shield and Tom as well.

Malvel had won. There was nothing more Tom could do.

CHAPTER TEN

VICTORY?

THE WATER SWIRLED AS ELENNA SWAM IN front of Tom, his sword gripped in one hand, her knife in the other. Fearlessly, she plunged the sword into Zepha's open mouth, jamming his beak open. The squid's eyes flared with anger. He released his grip on Tom and flung all his tentacles at Elenna. More bubbles escaped from her mouth as she gasped in alarm. She turned and swam away.

Tom knew he didn't have much time. The sword wouldn't hold Zepha back for long and he couldn't hold his breath much longer. He had to find the helmet, but in the battle with the squid he had lost his sense of direction. He peered down through the gloom, but he couldn't see the telltale glint of gold.

To his relief, Sepron came gliding through the greenish darkness. Tom could tell he had recovered his sight: His eyes glared with anger and he was heading straight for Zepha. He swooped down and wrapped his rainbow-colored coils around the squid. This time, Zepha couldn't squirt ink into his face, or grip him with his tentacles.

Sepron clutched the giant squid tighter and tighter with his coils. Tom could hardly believe what he was seeing. It looked as if the sea serpent was squeezing the life out of Zepha. Astonished, Tom watched as the edges of the squid started to blur. He looked around for Elenna, who had reappeared, and pointed frantically. Something was happening! Rippling movements came from beneath Zepha's skin as the evil Beast writhed in agony.

Suddenly, the monster squid's three pulsing, red hearts shattered into tiny glinting pieces,

too many for Tom to count, and his skin burst open, tearing cruelly. Tom struggled not to gasp as thousands of tiny squids shot out, swimming as if terrified. Zepha's empty papery skin began to sink slowly down into the gloom, toward the seabed. Malvel's beast was no more.

Elenna grabbed Tom's sword before it could fall out of sight. Tom swam after her, gazing around for a glimpse of the helmet. Then he spotted its golden gleam.

But exhaustion made his limbs heavy. He had no air left. His lungs were screaming with pain. Elenna must be feeling the same. Were they going to die after all?

Then Tom caught sight of Sepron swimming toward them. The sea serpent dove underneath them and rose slowly upward so that Tom and Elenna could cling to his scaly neck as he headed for the surface. Tom hugged Sepron with relief.

As they passed the coral spire where the golden helmet rested, Tom reached out and grasped it by the hooked beak.

Sepron's neck rose out of the water just beside the boat. Tom and Elenna hung on for a moment more, gasping air into their tortured lungs. Silver sprang up and rested his front paws on the side of the boat, letting out an astonished yelp.

Then the sea serpent lowered his neck, gently depositing Tom and Elenna into the bottom of the boat. Silver pushed up close to Elenna, nosing her. She rolled onto her back and allowed the wolf to lick her face. Her chest rose and fell as she gasped for air. Then she reached out a hand to ruffle Silver's fur. She was all right.

"Thank you, Sepron," Tom panted, reaching up to pat the serpent's gleaming scales. "We couldn't have done it without you."

Sepron bowed his head before sinking back beneath the waves again. Tom caught a last glimpse of his rainbow coils as he swam away into the open sea. He felt warmed by the thought that the Beast who had once been his foe had saved their lives.

"Well," he said with an exhausted sigh. "We've got the helmet."

"Why don't you try it on?" Elenna asked, climbing to her feet.

Tom hesitated for a moment, turning the helmet over between his hands. The gold shone brightly and he could see how skillfully the helmet was crafted — even the finest pieces from his uncle's forge couldn't compare.

Could it really be for him? Was he worthy to wear the helmet that had once belonged to the Master of the Beasts of Avantia?

"Go on!" Elenna urged him.

Tom raised the helmet and put it on his head. Instantly he felt it shrink to fit him. He gasped. His eyesight had suddenly grown stronger! He could see the people on the shoreline; Calum's father Matt was mending a fishing net and Lindon was squatting by the fire, drinking something from a bowl. Farther away from the sea, Calum was leading Storm along the edge of the trees. Tom could even see the whites of the stallion's eyes as he paced up and down.

"This is amazing," he exclaimed. "I can see everything! I just wish my father could see me."

"He'd be so proud of you," Elenna told him.

Triumph bubbled up inside Tom. The first part of his new Quest was over! He had retrieved the helmet. And now he was determined that it wouldn't be long before he found the other five parts of the armor, too.

"We've only just started," he said to Elenna. "I'm not giving up until I have every piece of the golden armor."

Elenna smiled in agreement. "Let's get back to shore," she said gently.

She pulled up the sail and began to guide the boat back to the beach.

They were halfway back when a familiar blue glow began to appear before them, and Aduro seemed to stand on the waves.

But this time he was not alone.

Behind him was Malvel, who held a slim dagger against the wizard's neck. Aduro's face was set hard. Tom knew that face: It was the one he wore himself when refusing to show fear.

"Get away from him!" Tom shouted at Malvel.

The Dark Wizard smiled. "So you have the golden helmet," he sneered. "But I don't suppose you feel quite so pleased with yourself now, do you?"

"I don't believe this!" Tom cried. "It's just an illusion. You could never take Aduro prisoner. You haven't the power."

"I'm afraid I do." Malvel dug the point of the dagger into Aduro's neck. "Tell them, fool."

"This is a true vision," Wizard Aduro said

reluctantly. "I was foolish, and didn't guard myself well enough. I am Malvel's prisoner."

"I'll free you!" Tom said defiantly.

Malvel laughed cruelly. "You can try."

Tom reached out to Aduro, but his hand passed through air. "Tell me what to do!"

"You must find the full suit of armor. . . . It is the only way."

Malvel let out a piercing laugh. "That will never happen. You'll fail the next test, Tom, when you have to face my second evil Beast — Claw."

"We'll do it," Tom vowed. "We'll free Aduro and destroy you once and for all."

"I can hold out against him," Aduro insisted, though his face was pale. "It is the Quest that matters now!"

Malvel's laughter rang out again as the vision faded.

Tom and Elenna exchanged a horrified glance. All of Tom's sense of triumph had vanished.

He could only think about Aduro in Malvel's clutches.

As they beached the boat, Calum came up to them, leading Storm. Tom had been wondering how to explain to Lindon why they had taken his boat without permission, but thankfully, the fisherman was nowhere in sight. Tom climbed out of the boat and took the stallion's reins, stroking his nose.

"Thanks," he said to Calum. Glancing out to sea again, he added, "I don't think you'll have any more trouble."

Calum met his gaze steadily. "I won't ask questions," he said. "You saved us once before, and that's good enough for me." He bent to give Silver a pat. "You're welcome to come and stay with my family if you'd like."

"Thank you, but we can't," Tom said regretfully. "We have other duties."

"I understand," said Calum. "But I hope you'll

come back when you can. You'll always find friends here."

Taking up his sword and shield, Tom climbed into Storm's saddle with Elenna behind him.

"Farewell!" Elenna called.

"Farewell, and good luck!" Calum replied.

With a last wave, Tom and Elenna headed up the beach to find the road that led back inland.

Tom felt as if a huge weight was pressing upon him. "This is our most important Quest yet," he said.

"I know." Elenna tightened her arms around his waist. "This time we've *got* to succeed."

Tom nodded. She was right. The Quest wasn't about his need to prove himself, not any more. It wasn't even about the magical golden armor.

It was about rescuing Aduro.

Could they do it?

"While there's blood in my veins," Tom swore, "I'll never give up!"